I want to dedicate this book to my children,

Maddie and Dawson.

When I grow up, I want to be just like them!

Special Thanks

Thank you to God, for without His love and grace, this book would not exist.

An enormous thank you to my parents for a lifetime of encouragement and support in **all things Lisa**.

Thank you to Parker Buhrman for his willingness to embark on an adventure with me without hesitation.

A special thank you to Judi, the first person who taught me sign language. She demonstrated such beauty in communicating with her hands.

This book was inspired by the following people:

Struggling readers who benefit from repetition of text, along with the simple enjoyment of a true childhood story.

Intervention specialists all over the world who can't help but believe that all children can learn to read.

Anyone with a disability who refuses to allow that particular disability to interfere with advancing in life. My illustrator is a perfect example of this!

Acknowledgments

Josie and the Toad
Copyright © 2023 by Lisa Hildebrand
Illustrated by Parker Buhrman
Published by Lucid Books in Houston, TX
www.LucidBooks.com

ISBN: 978-1-63296-573-8 (paperback)
ISBN: 978-1-63296-574-5 (hardback)
eISBN: 978-1-63296-575-2

JOSIE and the TOAD

BASED ON A TRUE STORY

LISA HILDEBRAND

ILLUSTRATED BY PARKER BUHRMAN

Hi! My name is Dawson.

I live with my family in the country.

I have a mom, a dad, and an older sister, Maddie.

Our house is away from the city on Fenner Road.
We have a creek and woods behind our house.
I love living in the country!

Meet our dog, Josie.

Josie is very playful and friendly.

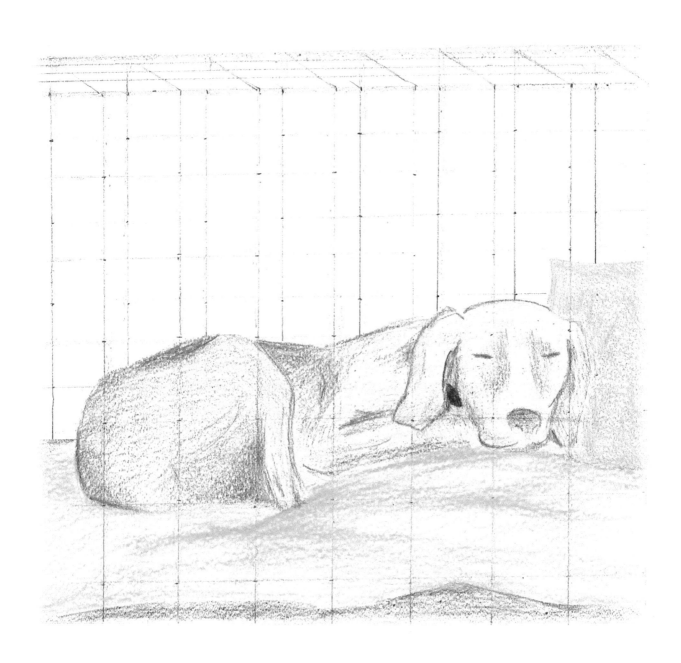

Josie has been crate trained.
Crate trained means that when we are
asleep at night, she likes to sleep in her crate.
It's like she has her own bedroom.

Sometimes, in the middle of the night,
Josie has to go to the bathroom.
That means my mom wakes up and
has to let her out in the yard.

One night, my mom was walking through our house and was startled to find a HUGE toad in the middle of our living room! Once she realized it was just a toad, she picked him up and put him outside.

A few nights later, my mother found the SAME
toad in the hallway! Again, she put the toad
outside and began to wonder how the toad
was getting into the house.

My mom started to crawl on her hands and knees, checking every area in the house, trying to figure out how the toad was coming into our home.

Over the next couple of nights, my mom found the toad over and over and over again. But she never figured out how it was getting in! It was driving her crazy. . . Finally, she figured it out.

Josie had to use the bathroom one night, and when
my mom went to let her back in the house . . .
she noticed little legs hanging out of Josie's mouth.

"That's it!" yelled Mom. Josie had been bringing the toad into the house by carrying it in her mouth! Once she got in her crate, Josie would release the toad, and then it would hop all through the house!

Josie and the toad became very good friends.
She wasn't allowed to bring it into the house anymore,
but they would sit together on the back porch.
They both enjoyed the warm sun.

┌─About the Author ─────────────────

Lisa is a wife and mother of two who lives in Ludlow Falls, Ohio. She graduated from Slippery Rock University with a BA in both Special Education and Elementary Education and has spent the last 26 years working in the area of special education. Lisa is a lover of all things for children. When she's not at work, she can be found kayaking, reading a book, or riding her bike. She also spends countless hours trying to convince friends and family to try something new with her, such as learning to play the ukulele, sleeping in a floating tent, eating at a new restaurant, or cardio drumming! Lisa enjoys organizing events and volunteering whenever possible at church and community events.

┌─About the Illustrator ─────────────

Parker and his high school sweetheart, Olivia, were born, raised, and continue to reside in Arcanum, Ohio. He has always had a love for the arts and a creative mind that never seems to shut off "new ideas." Parker loves to draw and sketch the images that pop into his brain. Parker was born with colorblindness and has found that he enjoys the challenges that come along with bringing these images to full color. When he's not illustrating or working his day job in the business world, he can likely be found renovating their 1800's home, working on projects in his barn, making music with his friends, or planning his next big road trip across the country.

Join us for more information and fun on Fenner Road at
www.misslisabooks.com